AuthorHouse™
1663 Liberty Drive
Bloomington, IN 47403
www.authorhouse.com
Phone: 1 (800) 839-8640

Published by AuthorHouse 12/20/2017

ISBN: 978-1-5462-1639-1 (sc)
ISBN: 978-1-5462-1637-7 (hc)
ISBN: 978-1-5462-1638-4 (e)

Library of Congress Control Number: 2017917217

Print information available on the last page.

This book is printed on acid-free paper.

authorHOUSE®

The Happy Penny

JENETTE DUHART

Illustrated by Joshua Allen

There was once a penny whose name was Penny Penny. He played with his friend Sue Penny.

Penny Penny and Sue Penny attended the same school. The name of the school was the School for Money.

Penny Penny and Sue Penny played together because all the other money made fun of them, laughed at them and pushed them around. The others told them they were of no value, and that made them feel very little.

"A penny has no value, unlike the other money," they said.

The other money just laughed and laughed at them.

They told Penny Penny and Sue Penny they needed to make friends with the other money so they could be of more value. Then they would have valuable friends, and that would make them valuable.

Penny Penny and Sue Penny felt very sad because the other money said the penny had no value.

9

Every day Penny Penny and Sue Penny went home crying; they did not know how to tell their parents that the other money at school said a penny had no value.

One day Penny Penny came home crying, and his parents asked him what was wrong.

He said, "Mom and Dad, am I of no value because we are pennies? All the other money has more value than we do. So they make fun of us and bully us. Is it true that we have no value?"

His mom replied, "No! That is not true, son; there is a lot of value in a penny. I think that we as your parents need to go to the school and talk about this. We will tell Sue Penny's parents as well. A penny can do what other money cannot."

The next day, Penny Penny's and Sue Penny's parents went to school with them to talk to the principal.

They let the principal know that Penny Penny and Sue Penny were having problems at school and that the other money was bullying them because they were pennies, that the other money told them that they were of no value because a penny has no value compared to the other money.

The parents told the principal that it should be stated that a penny has a lot of value and that it was urgent that the other money know this.

So the next day, Mr. Fifty Cent, the principal, had a special assembly about the value of money.

Mr. Fifty Cent said, "We are having a little misunderstanding. This is a school for money. The lowest coin in value is the penny."

"Did you all know that five pennies can make a nickel? And ten pennies can make a dime, twenty-five pennies can make a quarter, fifty pennies can make one-half dollar, one hundred pennies can make a dollar, and so on. A penny can make any coin or paper money, but no other coin or dollar bill can make a penny. Isn't that *remarkable*?"

PENNIES!

This made Penny Penny and Sue Penny and all other Pennies very happy; they were happy pennies now because they knew they were valuable!

Like Penny Penny and Sue Penny, we all have different qualities; we are unique and valuable.

Be yourself—you are very, very valuable!

Be happy like Penny Penny and Sue Penny!

I dedicate this book to London.

CPSIA information can be obtained
at www.ICGtesting.com
Printed in the USA
LVOW06s2309040118
561877LV00006B/13/P